Kate's Castle

By

Julie Lawson

Illustrated by

Frances Tyrrell

To Brittany,
Happy beach days!

Julie L

Stoddart Kids

Stoddart Publishing gratefully acknowledges the support
of the Canada Council and the Ontario Arts Council
in the development of writing and publishing in Canada.

First published in 1992 by Oxford University Press

Published in Canada in 1997 by Stoddart Kids,
a division of Stoddart Publishing Co. Limited
34 Lesmill Road
Toronto, Canada M3B 2T6
Tel (416) 445-3333 Fax (416) 445-5967
e-mail Customer.Service@ccmailgw.genpub.com

Published in the United States 1997 by Stoddart Kids
85 River Rock Drive, Suite 202
Buffalo, New York 14207
Toll free 1-800-805-1083
e-mail gdsinc@genpub.com

Canadian Cataloguing in Publication Data
Lawson, Julie, 1947–
Kate's castle

Poem.
ISBN 0-7737-5899-2

1. Children's poetry, Canadian (English).*
I. Tyrrell, Frances, 1959–
II. Title.

PS8573.A94K38 1997   jC811'.54   C97-930892-5
PZ7.L38Ka 1997

Printed and bound in Hong Kong by
Book Art Inc., Toronto

To my husband Patrick, with love.
— J.L.

For Marilyn
— F.T.

This is the castle that Kate built.

This is the moat of sandy hue
That circles the castle that Kate built.

These are the mussels, purple and blue,
That edge the moat of sandy hue
That circles the castle that Kate built.

This is the pool of anemones
Whose swaying tentacles comb the seas
That fill the moat of sandy hue
That circles the castle that Kate built.

This is the starfish, so hard to please,
Who gardens the flowery anemones
And polishes the mussels, purple and blue,
That edge the moat of sandy hue
That circles the castle that Kate built.

This is the tower of treasurely finds—
Moon snails and agates and sea urchin spines—
Kept in the castle that Kate built.

This is the staircase of twisting shells
That twirl and swirl in spiralling curls
Way up to the tower of treasurely finds—
Moon snails and agates and sea urchin spines—
Kept in the castle that Kate built.

Windows of sea glass, softly green,
Let in the light with a misty sheen
To shine on the staircase of twisting shells
That twirl and swirl in spiralling curls
Way up to the tower of treasurely finds—
Moon snails and agates and sea urchin spines—
Kept in the castle that Kate built.

This is the whale, sunlit and free,
Who leaps and splashes far out at sea,
Then sets his sail with a flip of his tail
To visit the castle that Kate built.

This is the snail, timid and shy,
Who guards the tower with watchful eye,
And waits for the whale who sets his sail
To visit the castle that Kate built.

This is the fish with the shimmery tail
Who teases and tickles the timid snail
Who guards the tower of treasurely finds—
Moon snails and agates and sea urchin spines—
Treasures to lure the princely whale
Who visits the castle that Kate built.

This is the sea that claims for its own
The golden castle that Kate calls home,
Floods the moat of sandy hue,
Flows over the mussels all purple and blue,

Sifts the sand in violet strands,
Swishes the shells with the setting sun
And sweeps the treasures one by one
Way out to the whale with the gleaming tail
Who visits the castle that Kate built.

And now the sand is moon-drenched and bare;
A silent mermaid combs her hair,
Watching the ebb of the restless tide,
She waits for another sun to rise
When Kate will gather new treasurely finds—
Moon snails and agates and sea urchin spines—
And build another castle of sand.
The castle of sand that Kate built.

Kate's Castle